THIS BOOK
BELONGS TO

D1344364

Hope the RAINBOW Fairy

Concept by Holly Lansley * Created and Designed by Jane Horne
Written by Rosie Greening * Illustrated by Lara Ede

make
believe
ideas

Hope the RAINBOW Fairy

worked her **magic** day and night

to spread nice **rainbow colours** and make **Fairyland** look bright!

 **Yellow** for
the **sunshine**

and **green**
for every **tree**,

then a hundred other
colours only
fairy eyes can see.

But then one year, a fairy flu
began to slowly spread.
"We need a plan to beat this!"
all the sneezing fairies said.

ATCHOO!

Soon enough, Hope heard the news
of what they had to do . . .

EVERYONE MUST STAY AT HOME TO KEEP SAFE FROM THIS FLU!

So every fairy, young and old,
stayed tucked up in their house,

and soon the whole of Fairyland
was quiet as a mouse.

But Hope began to worry.
The fairies needed cheer,
and it seemed the trees and flowers
would be colourless this year!

She opened her computer,

then she rang her friends and said:

"There won't be any COLOURS if I stay at home instead!"

Hope's friends said, "Don't worry, everyone will understand." But Hope knew that she had to try and **help out** Fairyland.

So Hope began to brainstorm ways
to spread JOY from her home,
and help the magic fairies
feel a little less alone.

She sent out **rainbow** ice lollies
for everyone to eat,

but they melted in the mail
and left big puddles in the street.

She set up lots of online games for everyone to play,
but the Wi-Fly soon cut out and it confused Gran anyway!

Finally, Hope waved her wand
to wish the flu away.
But she didn't have the power:
it seemed flu was here to stay.

"This is bad," cried Fairy Hope.
"I can't fix the flu,

but I can't spread colour either,
so what's left for me to do?"

Hope flew sadly to the roof.
"I miss my friends," she said.
Then, as she gazed at Fairyland,
a plan came to her head . . .

She whooshed her wand above her and, as quickly as can be,
a rainbow shone above her house for everyone to see!

One by one, the fairies saw the rainbow far away. The colours made them hopeful when so much felt sad and grey.

So the fairies got to work to make big
rainbows of their own.

It made them feel much better
now they knew they weren't alone!

Soon, each house in Fairyland had **rainbows** shining bright.
Each time the fairies saw them,
they knew things would be alright.

And Hope was thrilled that Fairyland
had more **colour** than ever.
The fairies were **connected**:
safe at home, but still **together**.

THANK YOU

The weeks went by in Fairyland,
until Hope heard one day . . .

THE FAIRY FLU
IS OVER—YOU
CAN MEET AGAIN
AND PLAY!

Hope flew from her house
and all the fairies gave a cheer.
They told her they were grateful
for the joy she'd brought that year.

So, even when the world seems grey,
there's colour we can share.

With kindness and community,

hope is always there.